DiNOSAUR

Land

Th great Escape!

ise
ast

M.J.MISRA

EGMONT

Books in the Dinosaur Land series

The Magic Fossil

Double Trouble!

Lost in the Wild!

The Great Escape!

For Thomas and Alexander Mullen,

my wonderful nephews.

EGMONT
We bring stories to life

Dinosaur Land: The Great Escape!
First published in Great Britain 2012
by Egmont UK Limited
239 Kensington High Street
London W8 6SA

Text copyright © Michelle Misra and Linda Chapman 2012
Illustrations copyright © Artful Doodlers 2012

ISBN 978 1 4052 6173 9

1 3 5 7 9 10 8 6 4 2

www.egmont.co.uk
www.michellemisra.com

A CIP catalogue record for this title is available from the British Library

Printed and bound in Great Britain by CPI
Group (UK) Ltd, Croydon, CRO4YY

51208/1

MIX
Paper
FSC   FSC® C018306

EGMONT LUCKY COIN

Our story began over a century ago, when seventeen-year-old
Egmont Harald Petersen found a coin in the street.

He was on his way to buy a flyswatter, a small hand-operated
printing machine that he then set up in his tiny apartment.

The coin brought him such good luck that today Egmont has
offices in over 30 countries around the world. And that lucky
coin is still kept at the company's head offices in Denmark.

CONTENTS

CONTENTS

Old Friends

'Max! Over here!'

Max Jordan saw his dad, who was standing with the other parents, waiting to pick him up from school. It was the end of the day and the playground was full of noise and excited chatter.

Max walked over slowly.

'Good day?' Mr Jordan asked.

'Not really,' Max said with a sigh.

'It can't have been that bad,' his dad said. 'You practised for that spelling test till you were blue in the face!'

'It's not the spelling test,' Max said quietly. 'It's . . . it's Josh . . . he's leaving the school, Dad! He's moving away!' Max looked down, trying to hide how upset he was.

'Oh dear . . .' Max's dad gave him an

understanding look. Max and Josh had been best friends since nursery. 'Are you all right?' he asked.

'Not really,' Max said quietly.

'Come on,' his dad replied. 'Let's go to the car. I have something that might cheer you up. It's the latest *Dinosaur Mania* magazine.'

Max managed a smile. He loved dinosaurs and *Dinosaur Mania* was his favourite magazine.

Mr Jordan led the way to their battered

old Land Rover. Max got in, trying to find space to sit amongst the books and empty medicine bottles that were scattered around. His parents were vets so the car was always full of bits and bobs.

Max put his seatbelt on and wound the window down. A shout came from nearby and a boy with a freckled face and a wide grin came running over.

'Hey, Max, are you going to football practice this evening?'

'Not today, Giles,' called Max.

Giles's mum followed him over. 'So *you're* Max. I've heard a lot about you.' She turned to Mr Jordan. 'I'm Jane Church. We're new here. Giles has just started at the school.'

'I'm Peter Jordan,' said Max's dad, shaking her hand. 'Pleased to meet you.'

'Maybe Max would like to come over for tea next week,' Mrs Church said.

'I'm sure he'd love that, wouldn't you, Max?' Mr Jordan replied.

'Yes, er, thanks.' Max hesitated. He wasn't sure what he'd have to talk about with Giles.

As Giles and his mum walked off, Mr Jordan got into the driver's seat. 'See, you make new friends easily,' he said. 'Giles seems to like you.'

'But he's not like Josh,' said Max. 'He's really into football and . . . and . . .'

'And?' Max's dad raised his eyebrows.

'And he doesn't like dinosaurs,' Max finished gloomily.

Mr Jordan laughed. 'That's not a good reason not to spend time with someone.' He glanced at Max. 'I think you should give him a chance. You don't always have to be friends with people exactly like yourself.'

'Mmm.' Max wasn't sure that he agreed. The reason he liked being friends with Josh was because they were *so* alike. They both knew the difference between hadrosaurs and lambeosaurs. They both liked the allosaurus more than the T-Rex and *Ice Age* was their favourite film.

His dad gave him a kind look. 'Hey, cheer up. Remember I said I had *Dinosaur Mania* for you? Here it is.' He pulled a magazine off the front seat and passed it over.

'Thanks, Dad!' Max said. There was a picture of an allosaurus on the cover. Its mouth

was open and it was showing all its teeth. Max couldn't wait to get home to start reading the magazine.

'Now, we'd better go,' his dad went on. 'I said we'd help Mum tidy up the surgery.'

Max groaned. He loved helping at the surgery, and going on the evening rounds to check on the animals was brilliant. But clearing up? That was definitely not top of his list of favourite things!

'I know you don't like tidying up,' said

Mr Jordan. 'But Mum's been working hard. She deserves a rest.'

'OK.' Max started to smile. 'Actually, clearing up reminds me of something.'

'Is it one of your jokes?' asked Mr Jordan, a twinkle in his eye.

Max nodded. 'What do you call a dinosaur that smashes everything in its path?'

Mr Jordan raised his eyebrows. 'I don't know. What *do* you call a dinosaur that smashes everything in its path?'

'Tyrannosaurus wrecks!' Max grinned. 'Get it?'

Mr Jordan chuckled. 'You and your dinosaur jokes, Max!' He turned the key in the ignition. 'Now, let's go home.'

It didn't take them long to drive home. Once they were there, Max jumped out of the car, ran to the back door of the house and let himself in. The sweet smell of cooking was the first thing to hit him. He was starving!

But after a quick hello to his mum, he hurried into the surgery to help his dad.

When they had finished, Max went back inside for tea. It was his favourite – sausages and mash! Max gobbled his food down, then he excused himself and hurried into the garden. It was still warm outside and he wanted to have a little time to himself. Getting the dinosaur magazine had cheered him up a bit, but he still couldn't help feeling sad about Josh.

Oh, if only I could go to Dinosaur Land again, he thought. *That would make me feel better*.

Max felt excitement buzz through him. He had a magic fossil that could whisk him away to a land where dinosaurs still lived. He had met lots of real, live dinosaurs there! And he had made friends too – with a girl called Fern and her dad, Adam, who ran a sanctuary for sick dinosaurs. Max longed to see them again. But he had to wait until *they* needed him to help with something. Instinctively, he reached into his pocket and touched the fossil . . . but nothing happened.

Sighing, Max started to read. He read that the longest dinosaur, the seismosaurus, was as big as five double-decker buses, and the troodon – the most intelligent dinosaur – had the largest brain.

'What have you got there, Max?' his mum said, coming out to join him.

'*Dinosaur Mania*!' said Max, showing her the cover. 'Dad got it for me. I've just been reading a really cool article. Did you know that different types of dinosaurs used to help each other out? The gallimimus, which was a bit like an ostrich and had a good sense of smell but not such good eyesight, often used to live with the maiasaura, which had good eyesight but *not* such a good sense of smell. That way each of them could warn the other of predators coming their way.'

'That does sound brilliant,' Mrs Jordan said. 'But not as brilliant as getting your homework in on time!' She raised her eyebrows. 'Five more minutes out here then you really must come in.'

Max groaned, but he knew his mum was right. 'OK,' he sighed. He watched as she disappeared down the path and then buried his nose back in the article. The more he read now, the more he'd have to look out for when he next went to Dinosaur Land!

Max had just turned the page when he thought he heard a low humming noise. Was he imagining it? He gasped. Could the magic be working? He reached into his pocket and saw that the fossil was glowing. His fingers trembled with excitement as he traced the pattern on the spiral of the stone. He must be about to go to Dinosaur Land again!

Back to the Wild

Max span round in a rush of swirling colours, tumbling over and over until he landed with a bump. His head was spinning and his mind racing as the colours disappeared. He got to his feet and looked around. There were open plains as far as the eye could see and in the distance there was a smoking volcano.

He was definitely in Dinosaur Land!

'Max! You're here!'

Max turned to see a girl, about his own age, running towards him. She had dark, curly hair and brown eyes and she was wearing a cotton tunic with a belt. It was Fern!

Fern reached Max and grabbed his arm. 'Come quickly!' she said, and started to lead him off to the two white boulders that marked the entrance to the dinosaur sanctuary. 'You're just in time.'

'For what?' Max asked.

'To see Algie released back into the wild!' cried Fern.

'Algie?' Max repeated, thinking about the other times he had visited and the different dinosaurs he'd met. He wracked his brains, but he couldn't think of a dinosaur called Algie.

'Come on,' Fern giggled, tugging on his arm. 'You've really got to see him. He's the cutest thing. He's a lambeosaurus. A baby one!'

She set off at a run and Max charged after her. They passed ponds and swamps and paddocks and barns, until finally they came to the little white house where Fern and Adam lived. Next door, there was a pen with a young stegosaurus in it.

'That's Jessie,' panted Fern. 'She's hurt her tail. But hurry, let me show you Algie.'

In the enclosure next door, a small dinosaur was chasing his tail. He was about two metres tall with a deer-like face, two hind legs and two smaller front legs, like arms. There was a brown frill on the top of his head and he was striped in greens and browns. His whole body whipped and swished as he ran in circles. He finally came to a stop beside a

little trough of water. He lapped it up greedily as Max and Fern neared the enclosure. After a minute, he leaned back on his hind legs and lifted up his two front legs, like a puppy begging for a treat. Then he let out a loud blowing noise, and a giant spurt of water!

Max reeled back as the water hit him.

Fern burst out laughing. 'Algie, meet Max. Max, meet Algie!'

Max wiped the water from his face. He was drenched! But he didn't mind – he was

just so excited. 'What's wrong with Algie?' he asked. 'He doesn't look ill.'

'His leg was injured,' said Fern. 'It's only just healed, which is why he's ready to be released. The problem is, he's small and weak and his herd keep chasing him away. This is the third time it's happened. We're hoping that now his leg is better and he's a bit bigger and stronger, the herd will be nicer to him.'

'Poor thing,' said Max, watching the little

lambeosaurus leaping around the enclosure. 'Why are the rest of his herd being horrible to him?'

Fern looked sad. 'It often happens with plant-eaters. A weak member of the herd attracts dangerous meat-eaters, so the herd gets rid of the weak one to avoid being attacked. I really hope Algie will be OK this time because he won't be able to survive on his own in the wild.'

'So, you're here again, Max. Welcome

back!' a cheerful voice said from behind them.

Max swung round to see a tall man with dark curly hair and sparkling brown eyes. He was riding on a large dinosaur. It looked a bit like a small triceratops, with two horns sticking up towards the sky, but its third horn, on the end of its nose, curved downwards. It was an einiosaurus. It was wearing a rope bridle with reins leading from a bit in its mouth.

'Trixie!' Max grinned, rushing over to
the dinosaur. 'And Adam! How are you?'
He reached out to give the einiosaurus a
welcoming pat. The dinosaur gave a gentle
snort, in and out, like bellows.

'We're all fine,' Adam said. 'Come on. Hop aboard! It's time to let Algie go free!'

Max stood on a large boulder and climbed on to Trixie's back behind Adam. Once Fern had opened the gate to Algie's pen, she climbed up on the einiosaurus too. They watched Algie. He seemed surprised to be given a taste of freedom. He came out of his pen and sniffed the air. Then he was off, trotting excitedly down the path that led away from the sanctuary. Trixie and her

passengers ambled along behind him.

'Wow! This is brilliant!' Max smiled, remembering the first time he'd had a ride on Trixie. It hadn't been quite as smooth back then – he'd been convinced he'd fall off.

As the two dinosaurs moved away from the sanctuary, Max looked at the great open plains around him. Dragonflies flew in the air and pterodactyls swooped through the bright blue skies like giant blackbirds. Soon Adam was guiding Trixie off down a path and they entered the cool of a canopy of trees.

'Algie's herd is out in the east,' Adam explained. 'A bit of a way to go,' he said apologetically.

But Max didn't mind. He was enjoying himself, watching Trixie gently nudge the lambeosaurus on his way.

'Baaaaaa,' Algie answered every time he took a prodding. But he didn't seem to mind.

'It's a bit like rounding sheep,' Max called over his shoulder to Fern.

'Sheep?' she echoed in surprise.

'Sheep – you know, little white woolly things with black faces and not much common sense,' Max explained. 'We round them up with a sheep dog.'

'A sheep dog?' questioned Fern.

Max remembered that there were lots of animals in his world that Fern had never heard of. 'Don't worry,' he said to her. 'A dog's an animal like . . . well, it's like a small, furry dinosaur. We have lots of them.

They're very friendly and live in our houses. Some of them round up another type of animal called sheep.'

'Your world sounds very strange!' said Fern.

As they walked out of the vegetation, Max looked into the distance. There was a shimmering lake ahead and grazing around it was a herd of dinosaurs. They all had crests on their deer-like heads and round bodies and slim, horse-like necks.

'Lambeosauruses,' Max breathed, watching as the creatures raised their heads. They had clearly spotted their guests and, one by one, they scented the air, as if trying to detect whether there was any danger. Algie stopped a little way off and sniffed the air too. But then he trotted forwards again.

'So far, so good,' Adam said.

'Brilliant!' said Fern.

'I hope this works,' said Adam. 'This really is Algie's last chance. If the herd reject him again we're going to have to let nature take its course.'

'What? You mean let him wander round without a herd? He'll die!' said Max, shocked.

Adam sighed. 'It might seem harsh, Max, but we really can't keep taking him back into the sanctuary. I'm afraid it's the way life is out here in the wild. He's had three chances now.'

'But what if he needs more than three chances!' Max protested. 'Shouldn't you give every dinosaur as many chances as it takes?'

Adam hesitated, then shook his head. 'No, I'm afraid not. We have to draw the line somewhere.'

Max frowned. He couldn't believe that Adam was serious about this being the little lambeosaurus's last chance. As Algie approached the herd, Max held his breath. What was going to happen? *Oh, please let it all be OK*, he thought. *Please let the others accept him.*

'Come on,' murmured Adam. 'Let's follow on behind.'

Max could hardly bear to watch. The largest dinosaurs were standing at the edge of the herd, with the smaller ones in the middle. Max had read that larger dinosaurs formed a circle around the front and the sides of the herd to protect the young against predators trying to attack. It was cool to see it happening for real!

The biggest lambeosaurus, clearly the

leader, stepped forwards to investigate Algie.

A stillness settled across the herd as the male leader sniffed at Algie's skin. Fern grabbed Max's hand. Suddenly the leader whipped his tail round and thumped Algie with it. Algie jumped back. The leader started to paw the ground, letting out a loud, angry noise.

'Oh, no,' whispered Fern as all the lambeosauruses started pushing and nudging each other. Algie ran a bit further

off and watched in alarm.

Gradually the herd settled down again. Algie edged closer. Once more the leader walked out and snuffled him. To Max's relief, he seemed to accept Algie this time. The leader gave a snort and began to graze.

Algie hesitated and then put his head down to graze too.

'It looks like they're thinking of letting him join them,' said Adam, sounding relieved. 'We'll keep checking on him but for now we're done here. There's nothing we can do but wait.'

But just as they turned to go, a loud noise sounded in the distance. Max recognised it instantly. It was the cry of a dinosaur in pain.

Adam looked alarmed. 'Uh-oh. One dinosaur's safe, but another's in trouble!'

The Great Escape

Max, Fern and Adam looked around to see where the noise was coming from. There, in the distance, stood a dinosaur. It was greeny-brown in colour and about the size of an elephant. It had heavy, armoured plates running down the middle of its enormous back and its spiny tail swished from side to side as it stomped across the plains. It stopped a little bit away and looked them up and down.

Max knew exactly what kind of dinosaur it was – there was no need to be afraid of it.

It was a stegosaurus. Stegosauruses were usually very gentle unless they were attacked.

'Oh, no, not him again.' Adam sighed as the dinosaur bellowed even more loudly.

'You know him then?' asked Max.

Fern nodded. 'You could say that. He's always here. He keeps coming to this spot.'

'That's weird,' said Max. 'Maybe he's injured and is asking for help?'

'That would be the obvious answer,' said Adam, scratching his head. 'But we've checked him over and there's nothing wrong – he just seems to want to hang around here. He looks sad and he's very thin for a stegosaurus. I don't think he's eating properly.'

'He keeps bellowing like that,' explained Fern.

Adam frowned. 'We'd better take another look at him.'

They made their way on foot to where the stegosaurus stood, just by the opening to a canopy of trees. Trixie followed.

The stegosaurus didn't make any attempt to move as they got closer. It just let out another pitiful roar.

'Come on, fellow,' said Adam, reaching out his hand and letting the stegosaurus take a sniff.

'We've called him Red,' Fern said, turning to Max. 'After the red spines down the centre of his back.'

As Max and Fern waited, Adam circled the

stegosaurus. He ran a hand down each of the sturdy legs before finally coming to stand in front of the dinoaur's head and checking his nostrils.

'It's a mystery,' he said. 'There's not a cut or a graze. No swellings. I'd better just take a look at his droppings.'

Even though Max was dinosaur-mad he couldn't imagine wanting to check out some dinosaur poo!

Adam ran his hand through what looked

like a large pile of elephant dung. 'Well, all seems fine with his droppings. So what do we do now?' He looked thoughtfully at Red. 'All right. I'm not going to take any chances. I think we should take him back in.'

Max was glad they were going to do something to try and help the unhappy dinosaur. Fern looked pleased too.

'Maybe we can cheer him up when he's back at the sanctuary,' she said.

'It's strange,' said Max to Fern as Trixie

knelt down and they climbed back on. 'I've read a lot about stegosauruses and Red just doesn't seem to be behaving normally.'

'I know,' said Fern. 'They're not the brightest of dinosaurs but they're usually quite lively and they're known for being incredibly brave. They're usually really good at defending themselves, but this one doesn't seem to care. We've already taken him back to the sanctuary once. It's as though he's lost interest in everything.'

'Stegosauruses also like charging at things!' Max said. 'But Red doesn't look like he's about to charge at *us*!'

'So, let's get him back and check him out again,' said Adam. 'Are you ready for some dinosaur herding?'

'Oh, yes!' cried Max and Fern.

On the ride back to the sanctuary, Trixie had no trouble steering Red in the direction that they wanted to go. The stegosaurus's head hung low to the ground and he made sad rumbling bellows.

It wasn't long before they were back and had settled Red into an enclosure.

'I'll get him some food,' said Fern.

She ran off, returning quickly with armfuls of hay and some sugar-cane treats.

Red sniffed at the hay, but then turned away. Even when Fern reached out her hand with the treats, his mouth just brushed over them.

'It's no use!' Fern put the sugar cane back

in her pocket, feeling disheartened. Red plodded to the closed gate and paced up and down, looking out towards the plains.

'Come on, let's go inside,' said Adam. 'I'll check him over later. Right now I'm starving. I could do with some lunch!'

'Me too!' grinned Max.

It was cool inside the little stone house after the heat of the midday sun. Max was glad to sit down and have a cold drink. One thing

was for sure – taking care of dinosaurs was
thirsty work!

It wasn't long before Fern and Adam had
rustled up a tasty meal of fresh bread and
creamy cheese.

'This is delicious, thanks!' said Max as they sat down at the table and started to munch.

'So tell us, Max,' said Adam. 'How are things with you in your world?'

'Oh, you know . . .' said Max.

Before he knew it, Max was telling Adam and Fern everything that had been going on: about Josh moving away, and how his dad thought friends could be made easily.

Adam listened carefully, then nodded his head. 'He's right about one thing – friends come in all shapes and sizes. Look at you – who would have thought you would have been sent to us . . . from another world!'

'That's true,' said Max. But he knew

it wouldn't stop him missing Josh. For a moment his eyes prickled as he thought about his friend.

Suddenly they were all distracted by a loud crashing sound from outside.

'What's that?' Adam raced over to the doorway, with Max and Fern hot on his heels.

They flung open the door just in time to see what was making all the noise. A dinosaur was crashing through the fences and enclosures of the sanctuary, flattening everything in sight. And it wasn't just any dinosaur either.

'Red!' exclaimed Max. 'He's trying to get back out to the wild!'

An Unexpected Discovery

'Not again!' groaned Adam.

'We'd better go after him,' said Max.

'No,' Adam replied firmly. 'Let's finish our lunch first. We all need to eat and it's not like he'll go very far. He's sure to go back to the place we found him this morning. Leaving him for a while will give him a chance to calm down.'

Max knew that Adam was being sensible, but he was itching to get out and check that Red was OK. It was clear from the look on Fern's face that she felt the same. They both gobbled down their food at lightning speed. Finally, after they had finished and cleared up the table, they headed outside.

First, they went to Red's paddock to check the damage. It wasn't as bad as they had expected. Red had crashed through three fences, but it was nothing that hard work couldn't fix.

'Right then, let's go and find him,' said Adam.

They mounted Trixie and went on their way. It was boiling in the afternoon sun, and enormous flies buzzed around their heads. Max batted them away, worrying about Red. Was Adam right? Would the stegosaurus be back where they had found him earlier?

It wasn't a long journey and, sure enough,

Red was there in the same spot. Max didn't

know whether to feel relieved or anxious.

Something was *definitely* wrong now. Red let

out a loud noise and rubbed his leg with his

head.

'There's blood!' gasped Max. 'His leg is

bleeding badly.'

Adam jumped down and gently approached. 'That's a boy, easy does it. We've come to help you,' he murmured.

It was obvious what was the matter. When Red had smashed through the fences, he

had torn a chunk out of his leg. He sniffed miserably at the bleeding wound. Max felt very sorry for him.

'It's a nasty injury,' said Adam. 'We're going to have to take him back to the sanctuary. I'll put on a temporary dressing – yarrow plant should help stop the bleeding.'

He walked towards the trees, then, a few minutes later, he came back out of the forest, clutching a fern-like plant. 'You two should stand back. I need to press down hard on the wound and Red's not going to like it. Why don't you head into the shade to keep out of his way?'

Fern nodded and Max followed her into the canopy of trees. 'Why's Red acting like this?' he said.

'I don't know,' said Fern. 'It's really strange.'

Max puzzled it over. Usually he could work out what was wrong with dinosaurs, but he didn't have a clue when it came to

Red. Max heaved a sigh. Maybe he would think of something when they got back to the sanctuary.

'Let's see if we can find some more yarrow for Dad in case he needs it,' said Fern.

They went a bit further down the track. As they turned the corner, they saw a large mound ahead of them.

'What's that?' asked Max.

'I don't know,' said Fern, her forehead wrinkled in surprise.

Getting nearer, they saw that it was a dinosaur – another stegosaurus!

Max and Fern looked at each other and broke into a run. The giant beast was lying on one side and its eyes were closed.

Fern knelt down and touched it. 'Oh, Max! It's dead!' she said. Tears welled up in her eyes. 'Quick! Can you go and tell Dad?'

Max raced off to fetch Adam. When they arrived back, Adam bent down to the stegosaurus's neck and then nodded sadly.

'Yes, she's dead, I'm afraid. She must have died a few days ago.' He looked anxiously over his shoulder to check on Red, but thankfully he was standing still.

Max swallowed. It was a horrible thing to see. The poor stegosaurus.

'What did she die of, Dad?' Fern asked.

Adam scratched his head. 'It's strange. She hasn't been attacked – there aren't any wounds on her – so another dinosaur can't have killed her. I guess she must just have died of natural causes, or old age. It seems strange that other dinosaurs haven't come to eat her though.'

'Unless . . .' Max looked back out beyond the trees where Red was pawing the ground unhappily. Suddenly everything started falling into place. 'Unless Red has been protecting her,' Max realised.

'Of course!' Fern gasped.

'That's it, Max! You've got it!' said Adam. 'This stegosaurus must have been Red's mate. He's been coming here to watch over her body.'

Max bit his lip. Poor Red. It was good that they knew what was wrong with him now, but what could they possibly do to help?

Keeping Secrets

'We need to get Red back to the sanctuary,' said Adam. 'He's badly injured. We can't leave him out here on his own – he won't be able to defend himself.'

'We mustn't let him get attacked!' said Fern fiercely.

'But won't he just break out again if we

take him back?' asked Max.

'Not when his leg is so painful,' said Adam. 'And I'll put him in a more secure enclosure, just to be on the safe side.'

It was hard for them to persuade Red to leave but, in the end, with Trixie pushing and prodding at him and Fern, Max and Adam encouraging him, he finally made his way back to the sanctuary.

Max felt so sorry for Red as he limped along in front of them, his head hanging low.

He knew from all the books he had read that stegosauruses weren't pack or herd creatures. They lived in pairs. Without his mate, Red would be miserable.

As they arrived at the sanctuary, Adam stopped Trixie so Max and Fern could dismount. 'I'll get Red settled into his new pen. Meanwhile, can you get some antiseptic leaves to make some poultices for his wounds? Calendula is good. It's a little yellow flower found in rocks. Eucalyptus leaves would help too.'

'I know where we can find them,' said Fern. 'Just leave it to us, Dad. We'll get them, won't we, Max?'

'Definitely!' Max declared.

The sun was just starting to fall on the horizon as Max and Fern made their way to the forest.

'Which path should we take?' said Max, coming to a standstill.

'That one,' said Fern, pointing at the path on the right, overgrown with ferns and creepers, bushes and flowers. 'We're sure to find stuff there.'

They set off, falling into a worried silence. Max tried to break the gloom.

'Hey, what do you call a T-Rex with carrots in his ears?'

'Oh, Max,' groaned Fern. 'I'm not in the mood for jokes now.'

But Max wasn't giving up that easily.

'Anything you want! Get it? You can call him anything you want because he can't hear you!'

He looked at Fern. But she had stiffened and was staring into the trees.

'What is it?' Max asked, forgetting the joke as he watched Fern's eyes narrow.

'Over there,' she said. 'Did you see something move?'

Max couldn't see a thing. 'I don't think so . . .'

'I'm sure I saw something,' insisted Fern.

'There it is again!'

Max looked more closely to where Fern was pointing. There, in the distance, was a baby dinosaur, looking lost. Max's heart sank.

It was a lambeosaurus . . . one that they both knew very well.

'Algie!' said Fern. 'What's he doing here? He should be with his herd!'

The two friends looked at each other in dismay.

'He must have been chased out again,' said Max. They started towards the little dinosaur.

'Algie!' Fern called.

It was strange to see him there, in the dense vegetation. He looked very scared. Fern felt in her pockets. Luckily she still had some of the sugar cane that she had brought for Red earlier.

'Here, boy,' she crooned, not wanting to frighten him. 'Easy does it.'

The baby lambeosaurus gave a little bleat of recognition and stumbled over. He thrust his head in Fern's palms and munched on the sugar cane. It seemed to cheer him up. Soon he was gambolling around them, much more like his usual mischievous self.

'This really isn't good,' said Fern, shaking her head. 'If he's here on his own, the herd must have rejected him.'

'And your dad said it was his last chance,' said Max. 'What can we do?'

Fern raised her chin stubbornly. 'Well, whatever Dad says, we can't leave him here. A predator could easily get him.'

'Hmm . . .' A plan was beginning to form in Max's mind.

Their eyes met.

'Are you thinking what I'm thinking?' asked Fern.

'That we could sneak him back into the

sanctuary?' said Max.

'Exactly!' exclaimed Fern. 'There's a shed behind the barn. It's only used for storing rope. He could go in there. We can look after him until he's bigger and stronger and then try him with the herd again.'

'Your dad'll be really mad if he finds out,' said Max.

'We'll risk it,' said Fern, stroking Algie fondly.

Max nodded. 'Come on, let's get those

herbs for Red and sneak Algie back while your dad is busy fixing the paddock.'

Quickly, Max and Fern looked for the herbs. Algie stayed close by. It was almost as though he knew Max and Fern would help him.

It wasn't hard to find the eucalyptus leaves. There were eucalyptus trees growing everywhere! But the little yellow calendula flower was more difficult to find.

'It must be out of season,' Fern wailed.

Finally, just as they had given up hope, they found a rock sheltering a few of the daisy-like flowers. Max and Fern grinned at each other in delight. Grabbing a handful each, they made their way back to the sanctuary. Algie trotted along behind them.

'Come on then, Algie,' grinned Fern. 'Homeward bound!'

Stand off!

Luckily Adam was too busy repairing the fences to notice what Fern and Max were up to when they got back.

They took Algie into the little shed and put down some straw for him to lie on. They gave him a huge bale of hay to eat, then hurried over to Red's enclosure.

The stegosaurus's head was so low his nose was almost touching the ground. His eyes were dull. He looked like all the life had been drained out of him.

Fern showed Max how to make the poultices for the wounds, like her dad had taught her. They crushed the eucalyptus leaves and calendula petals with a stone, then they packed the pulp into large dock leaves.

Red didn't utter a sound as they tied the

dock leaves on to his leg.

'You know, I've been thinking,' said Max. 'Red's injuries aren't his real problem. What are we going to do about his loneliness?

'I don't know,' said Fern. 'It's not going to get any better, is it? When we release him, he's just going to keep going back to that spot and pining for his old mate.'

'I've got an idea!' said Max. 'How about we find him another mate!'

'Go on . . .' said Fern.

'Well, what about that young stegosaurus you showed me when I arrived?' Max said excitedly. 'They might get on.'

'That's a brilliant idea!' said Fern. 'Let's go and tell Dad. It's definitely worth a shot!'

Max and Fern found Adam hard at work, putting the finishing touches to the enclosures. He listened intently to what Max had to say.

'I guess it's worth a try,' he said. 'Jessie,

the other stegosaurus, is a sweet creature and she's so young she hasn't found a mate yet. Maybe she'll be just what Red needs. Let's give it a go.'

They hurried over to where Jessie stood in her enclosure, grazing happily.

'Hey, Jess,' Fern called in. 'We've got someone we want you to meet.'

They herded Jessie out of her pen and over to Red's enclosure. As they stopped at the gate, Red sniffed the air.

Adam opened the gate and Jessie trotted in. Max and Fern held their breath.

Jessie stopped and the two stegosauruses eyed each other. They had clearly never met in the wild before.

'Do you think it'll work?' asked Fern anxiously.

'Oh, I hope so!' breathed Max.

They watched as Red lumbered over and sniffed Jessie suspiciously.

'Well, at least it's not an outright

rejection,' murmured Fern as the two stegosauruses circled each other warily.

'I don't know.' Max had spotted the spines on Red's back rattling slightly. He was sure that wasn't a good sign.

Jessie gave Red a playful nudge.

With a loud bellow, Red opened his mouth and charged at her.

Startled, Jessie backed into a corner, breaking part of the fence. Red stomped off and then turned to face her, shaking his head as if threatening to charge her again.

'OK, easy now, boy,' said Adam, climbing
into the pen and bravely standing between
the two dinosaurs.

Red backed off some more. He clearly
didn't want to hurt the person who had been
helping him.

'I don't think this was such a good idea,'
Adam called to Max and Fern. 'Let's get Jessie

out of here.'

Fern opened the gate and Jessie

trotted out quickly as Red stomped

off to the far side of the pen.

'I think he wants to be on

his own,' said Adam. 'You two take

Jessie back to her pen and

I'll fetch some rope to

fix that fence for

now.'

Jessie seemed

just as happy as Red to get out of the enclosure. Fern and Max herded her back to her own pen and she hurried in.

Max sighed. He'd really hoped his plan would work. What could they do now?

Just then, a surprised yell rang out. It was Adam!

Max swung round.

Adam was standing in the doorway of the shed where Max and Fern had hidden Algie. Adam was staring inside.

'Oh, no!' gasped Fern.

The excited lambeosaurus came charging out, sending Adam flying.

'What's going on here!' Adam exclaimed, getting to his feet.

'We can explain,' spluttered Max, racing over with Fern.

But there wasn't time for that. Algie was now charging around the sanctuary. He skipped and jumped happily, dodging Fern and Max's outstretched arms. Swerving all over the place, he finally came to a stop by a

large pond and jumped in with a big splash.

'What is *he* doing here?' Adam asked in an exasperated voice.

'Oh, please don't be cross, Dad!' Fern burst out. 'We found him in the forest when we were looking for the herbs.'

'He'd been chased out of his herd again,' Max added.

'So you decided to bring him back here? I told you both he'd had his last chance!'

'I know,' said Fern. 'But we couldn't leave him out there and . . . and . . .'

'Oh, no!' Max interrupted. 'Look at Algie!'

The lambeosaurus had leaped out of the pond and was heading straight for Red's enclosure. The fence was still broken from where Jessie had backed into it, and before they knew it the little dinosaur had hopped over it and rushed in!

Adam, Fern and Max stood rooted to the spot. What was Red going to do now?

Unexpected Results!

For a second it felt as if everything was in slow motion. Algie frolicked over to Red and ran around his massive legs, sniffing him playfully.

The stegosaurus gave an angry snort and shook his spines. Lowering his head, he started to chase the lambeosaurus. But Algie

was very quick. Each time the stegosaurus

charged at him, the little dinosaur ducked

out of his way.

'He's going to get hurt!' exclaimed Adam.

'Come on!' said Fern. 'We've got to get

him out of there.'

'No!' Adam caught hold of her arm. 'It's too dangerous. Red's so cross now he might charge at us too.'

'But we can't just let Algie get hurt, Dad!'

Fern pulled her arm away. 'I'm going in!'

'Fern! Wait!' Max said suddenly. While Fern and Adam had been talking, he'd been watching Algie and Red and had noticed something about Red's body language.

'Red seems less angry,' Max pointed out. 'Look! His spines have stopped rattling and he's lifting his head more. He's looking at Algie. Looking at him properly.'

It was true. The stegosaurus had stopped and was staring at the small lambeosaurus.

'What's he doing?' asked Fern.

'I don't know,' said Adam slowly.

'I think it's going to be OK,' said Max. He could almost see the tension slowly ease from Red's enormous body.

The stegosaurus was blinking at Algie. Algie trotted over. Red lowered his head but didn't threaten to charge. He just gave a deep snort.

'Let's leave them in there together,' said Max suddenly.

'But that's madness!' protested Adam. 'They're totally different types of dinosaur.'

'It doesn't matter,' said Max. He thought about the article in the magazine he'd been reading, before he came to Dinosaur Land. 'Sometimes different types of dinosaur can be friends. Sometimes they can help each other and live together.'

'Hmm, I suppose that *is* true,' Adam said thoughtfully. 'Maiasauras and gallimimuses often live together, though I've never been able to work out why.'

Max knew why. 'It's because they have different abilities. One hears better and the other sees better, so they look out for predators in different ways. They help to protect each other. Different dinosaurs *do* get on together if they can work as a team.'

'Do you think Red and Algie will be able to be a team?' asked Fern uncertainly.

Max nodded. 'I think they might.'

Red had started lumbering after Algie

again but this time it was clearly a game. It was like they were playing chase! The big dinosaur had a new sparkle in his eye.

'I think they'll be able to help each other loads. Algie can be company for Red, and Red will protect Algie. Red doesn't need another mate – he just needs a friend.'

Adam smiled as the two dinosaurs met in

the centre of the enclosure and touched
noses. 'Well . . . it looks to me like he's
found one.'

The dinosaurs snorted and began
to graze happily together.

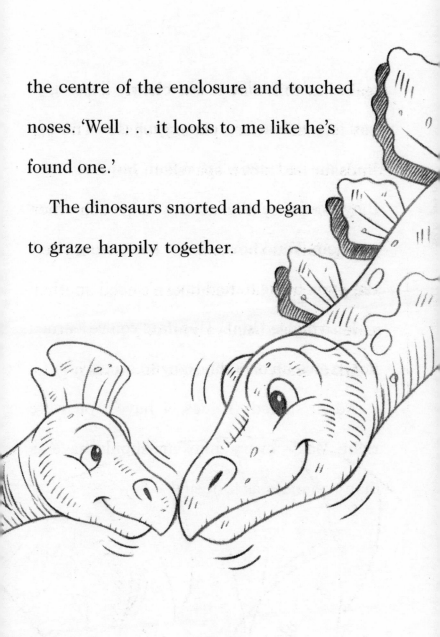

'Isn't this brilliant?' said Fern. 'I'm so glad you stopped us from separating them, Max.'

Adam nodded. 'I'd never have thought they could be the answer to each other's problem. You know, I learn something every time you come here, Max.'

Fern nudged him. 'This time you've learned not to give up on a dinosaur so quickly.'

Adam smiled. 'I guess I have. You were right, Max – every dinosaur should have as many chances as it needs!'

Max grinned. But he didn't have time to say anything as he heard a humming sound in the air. The magic fossil!

'I think I'm about to go home!' he cried, pulling the fossil from his pocket. It was glowing. 'Sorry I couldn't stay to see them being released!'

'Don't you worry about that, Max,' said Adam. 'Your work here is done!'

And with that, Max found himself whirling away in a sea of colours . . .

Max landed with a thud and rubbed his eyes. He was back in his garden, under the apple tree. The dinosaur magazine was spread out in front of him. He remembered what his mum had said before the fossil had whisked him away – five more minutes till homework. But such a lot had happened since then. He'd helped not just one, but *two* dinosaurs!

At that moment there was a shout.

'Max . . . Max, where are you?'

Uh-oh, that was his mum.

'You've got a visitor,' she called.

Max went into the house. He was surprised to see Giles in the hallway with his dad.

'We just dropped in on the way back from football practice,' Giles explained. 'I found this. You dropped it from your bag on the way out of school.' He held out a plastic dinosaur.

'Thanks!' Max breathed. 'I hadn't even noticed I'd lost it!'

'What sort of dinosaur is it?' asked Giles.

'A diplodocus,' said Max quickly. 'The dinosaur with the longest tail.'

'Imagine knowing that! That's brilliant!' said Giles. 'I don't know much about dinosaurs but I'd really like to learn.'

'Well, I'm sure Max will be able to tell you everything you want to know,' said Mr Jordan.

'Really?' Giles said hopefully. 'Will you, Max?'

As Max looked at Giles, something came

into his mind. Friends really did come in all different shapes and sizes.

'Of course I can!' Max grinned. He stopped for a moment to think about his friends back in Dinosaur Land. *What might they be up to*, he wondered. Then he turned back to his new friend.

'Come on, let's go and play dinosaurs!'